JF $2.95   C 1   Sp   Chi
H
Harwood, Pearl Augusta
The widdles

nc
749

THE WIDDLES

THE WIDDLES

By Pearl Augusta Harwood

Illustrated by Henning Black Jensen

Published by

Lerner Publications Company

Minneapolis, Minnesota

Mr. and Mrs. Widdle lived in a house by the sea in
Hawaii.

It was a very big house. It was a fine house.

It had a first floor, with a living room, a dining room,
and a kitchen. It had porches all around the outside.

It had a second floor on top of the first floor.

The second floor had five bedrooms and two bathrooms.

Mr. and Mrs. Widdle were glad to have such a big house.
But they lived in it all by themselves. They were LONELY.

Mr. Widdle was tall and thin, with straight dark hair. His eyes were green.

Mr. Widdle grew papayas and coconuts in his very large yard. He grew other things to eat in his very large garden. He kept his tools in his very large barn. He worked in his garden every day.

Mrs. Widdle was short and round, with curly brown hair. Her eyes were blue. Mrs. Widdle worked in her very large kitchen. She wore a checked apron. She made papaya juice and papaya jelly and papaya salads. She made coconut cookies and coconut pies and coconut cakes.

But there were no children to help them eat the jelly and the salads and the cookies and the pies and the cakes.

Mr. and Mrs. Widdle wished for some children to live in the very large house with them. They wished for some children to help eat the good things from the garden.

One day Mr. Widdle said, "Let us go to the orphans' home in the city. That is where they keep children with no mothers or fathers."

"Yes, yes!" said Mrs. Widdle. "Perhaps we can find a nice little girl with curly hair."

"About two years old," said Mr. Widdle.

The very next day, Mr. and Mrs. Widdle went to the orphans' home in the city. They wanted to look at the very small children there.

A boy met them at the door.

"Will you show us where the very small children are?" said Mrs. Widdle.

"Yes," said the boy. "I will get the lady who looks after the little ones."

"What is your name?" asked Mr. Widdle.

"My name is Lee Chan," said the boy.

"How old are you?" asked Mr. Widdle.

"I am eight years old," said the boy.

"Do you live in this home?" asked Mrs. Widdle.

The boy looked very sad. "I guess I will be here always," he said. "All the people who come for children want little ones."

"Oh no," said Mr. Widdle. "I am sure some people want boys just like you."

Lee Chan opened his black eyes very wide. "Do you know any people who want boys like me?" he asked.

Mrs. Widdle put her arms round about Lee Chan.

"I guess we *do* know some people," she said. "I guess *we* would like a boy just like you!"

"But you wanted a *little* boy or girl," said Lee Chan.

"I guess we can look for a little one some other time," said Mr. Widdle with a large smile. He took Lee Chan by the hand.

"Take us to the lady who will tell us all about you," said Mrs. Widdle. So Lee Chan did.

The lady said, "Lee Chan's mother and father were Chinese. Lee Chan is a Chinese American boy."

"That is just fine," said Mr. and Mrs. Widdle.

So Lee Chan went to live in the very large house by the sea.

He slept in one of the five bedrooms, next to Mr. and Mrs. Widdle.

He played on all of the porches. He played in the sand and in the sea. He helped Mr. Widdle in the gardens.

He went to school on the school bus which came right
past his house. He had new suits to wear, and wonderful
things to eat, and a bicycle to ride. His name was changed
to Lee Chan Widdle.

There was just one thing the matter.

Lee Chan Widdle was LONELY.

He missed the children at the orphans' home. Every night he looked at the three empty bedrooms.

He wished for a playmate to live in the very large house with him. Even a very little boy would be something to play with. Even a very little girl.

So one morning when he was eating papayas and coconut for breakfast, he said to Mr. and Mrs. Widdle,

"You said you would look for a very little boy or girl at the orphans' home sometime."

"Why, so we did!" said Papa Widdle.

"How could we forget!" said Mama Widdle.

"We will go to the orphans' home tomorrow," said Mr. Widdle. "Tomorrow is Saturday."

"Lee Chan can help us pick out the little one," said Mrs. Widdle. "A nice little girl with curly hair."

"Or a little boy with straight hair," said Mr. Widdle. "About two years old."

They all went to the orphans' home in the city. A boy met them at the door.

"Will you show us where the very small children are?" said Mr. Widdle.

"Yes," said the boy. "I will get the lady who looks after the little ones." He looked at Lee Chan and Lee Chan looked back at the boy.

"What is your name?" asked Mr. Widdle.

"My name is Yoshi," said the boy.

"How old are you?" asked Mr. Widdle.

"I am eight years old," said the boy.

"How long have you been in this home?" asked Mrs. Widdle.

The boy looked very sad. "I came here last week," he said. "I guess I will be here always."

"Why?" said Mr. Widdle.

"Because the people who come for children want *little* ones," said the boy.

"Oh no," said Mr. Widdle. "I am sure some people want boys just like you."

Yoshi opened his eyes very wide.

"They took *me*," said Lee Chan, and he took hold of Papa Widdle's hand.

"They took you from *here*?" said Yoshi.

Mrs. Widdle put her arms round about Yoshi. "Yes we did," she said, "And we will take you, too, to be a brother to Lee Chan."

"But you wanted a very *little* boy or girl," said Yoshi.

"I guess we can look for a little one some other time," said Mr. Widdle with a large smile. "Two boys, both eight years old, will be quite enough for now."

"Take us to the lady who will tell us all about you," said Mrs. Widdle. So Yoshi did.

The lady said, "Yoshi's mother and father were Japanese.

"How old are you?" asked Mrs. Widdle.

"I am eight years old," said the boy.

"How long have you been in this home?" asked Mrs. Widdle.

"I just came yesterday," said the boy. He looked very sad. "I guess I will be here always. The people who come for children want very small boys or girls."

"Oh no," said Mr. Widdle. "I am sure some people want boys just like you."

"They took *us*," said Lee Chan, and he took hold of Papa Widdle's hand.

Carlos opened his eyes very wide. "They took *both* of you, from *here*?" he said.

Mrs. Widdle put her arms round about Carlos. "Yes," she said. "And we will take you, too, to be a brother to Lee Chan and Yoshi."

"But you wanted a *little* boy or girl," said Yoshi.

"I guess we can look for a little one some other time," said Mr. Widdle with a large smile. "Three boys, all eight years old, will be quite enough for now."

"Take us to the lady who will tell us all about you," said Mrs. Widdle. So Carlos did.

The lady said, "The mother and father of Carlos came here from Puerto Rico. They were Spanish. Carlos is a Spanish American boy."

"That is just fine," said Mr. and Mrs. Widdle.

Carlos

Lee Chan

Yoshi

So Carlos went to live in the very large house by the sea.

The three boys played together on all the porches. They played in the sand and in the sea. They helped Mr. Widdle in the garden.

They went to school on the school bus. They all took turns riding the bicycle.

Carlos had a new last name. It was Widdle.

There was just one thing the matter.

The three boys felt just a little LONELY.

Papa and Mama Widdle had a bedroom. Lee Chan had a bedroom. Yoshi had a bedroom. Carlos had a bedroom. But there was one empty bedroom.

"There should be a very little boy or girl to sleep in that empty bedroom," said Carlos.

"Yes," said Lee Chan. "We could all help take care of a very little boy or girl."

"We could help every day," said Yoshi.

So one morning when they were all eating papayas and coconuts for breakfast, Carlos said to Mr. and Mrs. Widdle, "You said you would look for a very little boy or girl at the orphans' home sometime soon."

"Why, so we did!" said Papa Widdle.

"How could we have forgotten!" said Mama Widdle.

"We will go to the orphans' home tomorrow," said Mr. Widdle. "Tomorrow is Saturday."

"Lee Chan and Yoshi and Carlos can help us pick out the little one," said Mrs. Widdle. "A nice little girl with curly hair."

"Or a little boy with straight hair," said Mr. Widdle. "About two years old."

"We would like to see some very small children," said Mrs. Widdle.

"About two years old," said Mr. Widdle.

The lady smiled. "We do not have any two-year-olds right now," she said. "But we have *something* — that is just *one* year old today."

Mr. and Mrs. Widdle looked at each other.

"Is the something a little girl?" asked Mrs. Widdle.

"I will show you," said the lady.

She took them into a small room. In the room there were two beds. In the beds there were two brown babies, just exactly alike.

"Here are Lou Emma and Lou Etta," the lady said. "They need a home together, for they are twins."

"Twins!" said Mama Widdle. "With brown skin, and brown eyes, and dark hair!"

"You can braid it nicely in a few years," said the lady.

Lou Emma and Lou Etta both smiled, and held up their arms.

They had round faces, and dimples. They were very pretty.
Mama Widdle put her arms about them both.

"The mother and father of the twins were Hawaiian," the
lady said. "Lou Emma and Lou Etta are Hawaiian
Americans."

"That is just fine," said Mr. and Mrs. Widdle. "The Hawaiians were the first people in Hawaii."

Lee Chan and Yoshi and Carlos hopped around the babies.

"We will help you braid their hair!" said Lee Chan.

"We will help you feed them," said Yoshi.

"We will give them rides," said Carlos.

"This is just what we need for that empty bedroom," said Papa Widdle.